Engineering Our World
How a Submarine Is Built
I0822240
By Tanya Dellaccio
Gareth Stevens
PUBLISHING

Please visit our website, www.garethstevens.com. For a free color catalog of all our high-quality books, call toll free 1-800-542-2595 or fax 1-877-542-2596.

Library of Congress Cataloging-in-Publication Data

Names: Dellaccio, Tanya, author.
Title: How a submarine is built / Tanya Dellaccio.
Description: New York : Gareth Stevens Publishing, [2021] | Series: Engineering our world | Includes index. | Contents: Underwater Travels – Start with the Shell – Sink or Swim – Making Moves – Molding Metals – Nuclear Power – Alternative Energy – Submarine Technology – Make Your Own Submarine.
Identifiers: LCCN 2019030745 | ISBN 9781538247150 (paperback) | ISBN 9781538247167 (6 Pack) | ISBN 9781538247174 (library binding) | ISBN 9781538247181 (ebook)
Subjects: LCSH: Submarines (Ships)–Design and construction–Juvenile literature.
Classification: LCC VM365 .D355 2020 | DDC 623.82/05–dc23
LC record available at https://lccn.loc.gov/2019030745

First Edition

Published in 2021 by
Gareth Stevens Publishing
111 East 14th Street, Suite 349
New York, NY 10003

Designer: Sarah Liddell
Editor: Monika Davies

Photo credits: Cover, pp. 1, 5 noraismail/Shutterstock.com; background Jason Winter/Shutterstock.com; p. 7 CHARLY TRIBALLEAU/Staff/AFP/Getty Images; p. 9 Arterra/Contributor/Universal Images Group/Getty Images; p. 11 MAV Drone/Shutterstock.com; p. 13 FOTOGRIN/Shutterstock.com; p. 15 Daniel Gale/Shutterstock.com; p. 17 GLYN KIRK/Stringer/AFP/Getty Images; p. 19 AFP/Stringer/AFP/Getty Images; p. 20 (plastic tubing) krichie/Shutterstock.com; p. 20 (tape) bjphotographs/Shutterstock.com; p. 20 (rubber bands) Quang Ho/Shutterstock.com; p. 20 P Maxwell Photography/Shutterstock.com; p. 20 (water bottle) Shyripa Alexandr/Shutterstock.com; pp. 20, 21 Wanannc/Shutterstock.com; p. 21 (straw) Louella938/Shutterstock.com.

Printed in the United States of America

CPSIA compliance information: Batch #CS20GS: For further information contact Gareth Stevens, New York, New York at 1-800-542-2595.

Contents

Words in the glossary appear in **bold** type the first time they are used in the text.

Underwater Travels

Have you ever wondered what it's like to swim with fish and other sea creatures underwater? Submarines make it possible to find out! Submarines are big boats that are completely covered, which makes it safe for them to travel underwater.

Submarines were first created for military purposes and to use in battle. The vessels, or ships, would hide underwater and attack the enemy from below. Submarines are now used not only for the military, but for scientific **exploration** too!

Building Blocks

Architects are people who plan the shape of buildings and **structures**. Architects in the navy plan the shape of ships, like submarines! They start by drawing detailed plans of what they want the submarine to look like.

ENGINEERS ARE PEOPLE WHO USE SCIENCE AND MATH TO BUILD OBJECTS THAT HELP SOLVE SOCIETY'S PROBLEMS. SPECIAL TYPES OF ENGINEERS BUILD SUBMARINES.

Start with the Shell

As you go farther under the water's surface, water **pressure** becomes higher. Submarines need to be built to handle this pressure, while keeping the passengers, or people travelling inside, safe.

The majority of submarine structures are made of steel. Construction on a submarine often starts with two shell-like structures, called hulls. One hull is the outside, tube-shaped shell of the submarine. The second hull rests inside the first. This is where the submarine's passengers stay. Since steel is very strong, it's usually used to make the inside hull.

Building Blocks

The outside hull is strong, but the inside hull is a lot stronger and can handle the pressure deep below the water's surface. The inside hull is called the "pressure hull."

WOOD STRUCTURES ARE MADE IN THE SHAPE OF EACH HULL, AND BIG STEEL SHEETS ARE WRAPPED AROUND THEM TO CREATE THE CURVED SHAPE OF THE SUBMARINE.

Sink or Swim

Buoyancy is how well something floats in water or air. If something has positive buoyancy, it floats. If something has negative buoyancy, it sinks. Controlling a submarine's buoyancy is hard. Spaces between the two hulls help fix this problem.

After the hulls are in place, big tanks are placed in the space between them. These are called ballast tanks. Ballast tanks are what make it possible for submarines to float up to the water's surface or sink deep underwater.

Building Blocks

When air is brought into the ballast tanks, it makes the submarine lighter, which helps the submarine rise to the water's surface. Water is brought into the tanks to make the submarine heavier, which helps it dive down.

THIS IS A SUBMARINE'S CONTROL ROOM WHERE WATER FLOWS INTO BALLAST TANKS. THE TANKS ALSO HELP KEEP THE SUBMARINE "TRIM," WHICH MEANS THAT THE VESSEL IS BALANCED AND LEVEL IN THE WATER.

Making Moves

After the shell of the submarine is complete, many pieces are added to its exterior, or outside, to help control the submarine's movement. Pieces of metal shaped like fins, called diving planes or hydroplanes, are added. The fins move in different directions to help the submarine float up or sink down.

Submarines also have rudders, which are like diving planes. Once the submarine has reached the proper **submersion** level with the diving planes, the rudders help move the vessel side to side.

Building Blocks

Submarines sometimes have periscopes on their exterior. Periscopes are long tubes that stick out of the submarine's top. They have **prisms** connected to them to help people see what's on the surface of the water while the vessel is submerged.

IN THE PAST, MANY OF THE SUBMARINE'S CONTROLS COULD BE FOUND IN A CENTER TOWER, ALSO CALLED THE SAIL, BUT NOW THEY TAKE UP MORE ROOM AND ARE USUALLY FOUND IN THE HULL.

Molding Metals

Propellers help control the submarine's movement. The spinning propellers move the ship forward, and the rudders and diving planes move the ship in the right direction. They are powered by the ship's engine.

The ship's propellers, rudders, and diving planes are often made by sand casting. This is a method where sand is shaped and hardened into a mold, or a hollow form. Melted metal is then poured into that mold. When the metal hardens, the shaped rudders, diving planes, and propellers are what remain.

Building Blocks

Welders are people who specialize in heating and shaping metal to form structures. They are some of the many workers that help construct submarines.

SOME MILITARY SUBMARINES CARRY WEAPONS, OR OBJECTS USED TO FIGHT AN ENEMY, SUCH AS TORPEDOES, WHICH ARE TUBE-SHAPED EXPLOSIVES USUALLY FIRED UNDERWATER.

Nuclear Power

Keeping a submarine powered underwater is a tricky task. Submarines are usually powered two different ways.

Larger submarines, like ones for the military, mainly use nuclear power to move around underwater. Nuclear power is caused by splitting apart the **nuclei** of atoms, which are the smallest particles of a substance. This heats water and creates steam. The steam makes energy that then powers the engine. Nuclear-powered submarines can travel around 400,000 miles (664,000 km) without worrying about running out of power.

Building Blocks

Uranium is the element that makes nuclear power work. When uranium fissions, or its atoms' nuclei are split, energy is let out, starting a chain reaction that creates heat. That energy is then used to power submarines!

NUCLEAR-POWERED ENGINES DON'T NEED AIR TO WORK. THIS ALLOWS THE SUBMARINE TO SPEND MANY MONTHS UNDERWATER WITHOUT NEEDING TO SURFACE!

Other Energy Options

Submarines can also be powered by a mixture of electricity and diesel fuel, or gas. Electric engines often power smaller submarines used for scientific studies.

Diesel fuel is used to power the engine, but only when the submarine is near the water's surface. Fuel needs oxygen, or the colorless, odorless gas found in air, to produce energy. Once the submarine travels underwater, the vessel's engine instead gets power from large **batteries** stored inside the submarine. The batteries are continuously charged when the submarine is on the water's surface.

Building Blocks

Smaller submarines used for scientific studies are often attached to above-the-water ships which help them go underwater and get back to the surface.

THIS IS A SUBMARINE'S ENGINE ROOM. SUBMARINES THAT RUN OFF OF DIESEL FUEL CAN HAVE MORE THAN ONE ENGINE!

Submarine Technology

It's really dark far under the water's surface! Figuring out the right direction to go underwater is nearly impossible without the right **technology**. Modern submarines use sonar systems to find their way. Electrical engineers construct these systems.

Sonar systems are machines that use sound waves to find things in a body of water. Sound waves bounce off objects in the water, sending a sound that repeats back to the system. The system figures out how far away the object is based on how long the sound takes to return.

Building Blocks

The electricity on a submarine helps people breathe too. Oxygen **generators** on a submarine use electricity to form oxygen. Some submarines also have big tanks that let out fresh oxygen throughout the day.

THE SUBMARINER BELOW IS USING A SONAR SYSTEM. WHEN SUBMARINES ARE NEAR THE WATER'S SURFACE, THE VESSELS USE GPS TO FIND THEIR WAY.

Make Your Own Submarine

Now that you know how a submarine is built, you can build your own with a plastic bottle!

What You Need:

- plastic tubing (cleaned)
- modeling clay
- plastic bottle
- bendable straw
- rubber bands
- 6 pennies
- exterior painter's tape
- craft knife
- large bowl

How To Do It:

1. Ask for an adult's help poking a hole just big enough for your straw in the plastic bottle's cap. Your bottle acts as the outer hull of your submarine. Put the straw inside of the hole, bending it upwards, using the modelling clay to hold it in place. Attach the plastic tubing to the straw.
2. Lay your submarine on its side. Cut three small circles on one side of your plastic bottle using a craft knife. The holes are on the bottom of your submarine. These holes will act as your submarine's ballast tanks.
3. Tape three pennies together in a pile with painter's tape. Do that a second time with the other three pennies.
4. Use your rubber bands to connect the piles of pennies to the plastic bottle. Place one pile next to the front hole you cut in the plastic bottle. Then, place the second pile next to the back hole. The pennies shouldn't cover the holes.
5. Fill your large bowl with water and drop your bottle submarine in. Make sure the opening of your straw doesn't become submerged. Once your submarine fills all the way up with water, blow into the plastic tube. Does your submarine rise to the water's surface?

Glossary

battery: a device that turns chemical energy into electricity

exploration: the act of searching in order to find out new things

generator: a machine that uses moving parts to produce something, like oxygen

GPS: stands for Global Positioning System. A system that uses satellite signals to locate places on Earth.

nucleus: the central part of an atom made up of protons and neutrons. The plural is nuclei.

pressure: a force that pushes on something else

prism: a see-through glass or plastic object that usually has three sides and separates light

propeller: a device on a vessel with paddle-like parts that spin to move the vessel forward

structure: something built

submersion: the state of being put or sunk below the surface of water

technology: the way people do something using tools and the tools that they use

For More Information

Books

Gibbons, Gail. *Exploring the Deep, Dark Sea*. New York, NY: Holiday House, 2019.

Mattern, Joanne. *Submarines and Submersibles*. Vero Beach, FL: Rourke Educational Media, 2019.

Walt, Brody. *How Submarines Work*. Minneapolis, MN: Lerner Publications, 2019

Websites

Facts About Submarines
www.scienceforkidsclub.com/submarines.html
Find out more about the history of submarines and how these vessels work.

How Does a Submarine Work?
www.wonderopolis.org/wonder/how-does-a-submarine-work-2
Learn more about buoyancy and submarines here.

Submarine Facts for Kids
www.sciencekids.co.nz/sciencefacts/vehicles/submarines.html
Read more fun facts about submarines.

Publisher's note to educators and parents: Our editors have carefully reviewed these websites to ensure that they are suitable for students. Many websites change frequently, however, and we cannot guarantee that a site's future contents will continue to meet our high standards of quality and educational value. Be advised that students should be closely supervised whenever they access the internet.

Index